Buster Climbs the Walls

by Marc Brown

For Laura and Julia Severson

 LITTLE, BROWN AND COMPANY

New York ↣ Boston

Little, Brown and Company, Time Warner Book Group
1271 Avenue of the Americas, New York, NY 10020 • www.lb-kids.com
First Edition: September 2005
Library of Congress Cataloging-in-Publication Data
Brown, Marc Tolon.
Buster climbs the walls / Marc Brown.--1st ed.   p. cm.—(Postcards from Buster)
Summary: When his father takes him to visit Boulder, Colorado, Buster sends postcards to his friends
back home sharing what he is learning about the Rocky Mountains and rock climbing.
ISBN 0-316-15913-1 (hc)—ISBN 0-316-00126-0 (pb)
[1. Rock climbing—Fiction. 2. Rabbits—Fiction. 3. Postcards—Fiction. 4. Boulder (Colo.)—Fiction.
5. Rocky Mountains--Fiction.] I. Title. II. Series: Brown, Marc Tolon. Postcards from Buster.
PZ7.B81618Bjc 2005 [E]—dc22   2004018618
Printed in the United States of America • PHX • 10 9 8 7 6 5 4 3 2 1

All photos, except page 33, from *Postcards from Buster* courtesy of WGBH Boston and Cinar Productions, Inc.,
in association with Marc Brown Studios.

Do you know what these words MEAN?

belayer: (bee-LAY-er) a person attached to a rope who helps stop a climber attached to the other end of the rope from falling

bouldering: (BOHL-der-ing) a kind of rock climbing that involves climbing huge boulders or low cliffs

canyon: a deep valley with steep sides; often has water running through it

cliff-hanger: an adventure story in which every chapter ends at an exciting moment, so you can't wait to read the next chapter

foothold: a place where you can put your feet safely while climbing

harness: (HAR-nes) straps that fasten to a climber to help keep her safe

STATEtistics

Boulder, Colorado

- The Rocky Mountains are a mountain range that extends from Alaska to Mexico. The highest peak is Mt. Elbert in Colorado.

- The cheeseburger was invented in Denver, Colorado.

- Colorado means "colored red."

Arthur watched Buster put clothes into his suitcase.

"Buster, why do you have a pile of rocks in the corner?" Arthur asked.

"I'm going to the Rocky Mountains," Buster explained, "and I want to get used to the view."

Buster looked out the car window.

"So this is Boulder, Colorado," he said.
"I wonder where it got its name."

"Well," said his father,
"boulders are big rocks.
And there are plenty of those
around here."

Dear Arthur,

The Rocky Mountains really are rocky.

The highest peak is over 14,000 feet tall.

I don't know if they were called the Pebble Mountains when they were smaller. I will try to find out.

Buster

Arth
100
Elv

Buster saw some kids
playing on the rocks.

"Hi!" he said. "My name is Buster."

"I'm Wilson," said the boy.
"And this is Olivia, Lindsey, and Isabelle."

"You're all pretty good at climbing,"
said Buster.

"Oh, these rocks are easy," said Wilson.

"Why don't you come see
our favorite place?" said Olivia.

The next rocks were much taller. Wilson and Isabelle started climbing at once.

"That looks impossible," said Buster.

He found an easier way to the top.

"I feel sorry for everyone going up the side of the rocks," he said.

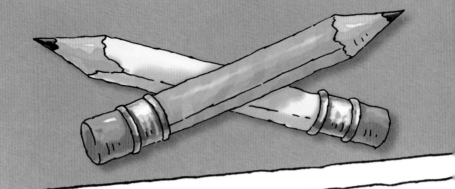

Dear Brain,

I visited my first canyon.
It was formed by a river
that cut deeper and deeper
into the ground.

This process takes thousands
and thousands of years.

Nobody builds canyons
in a hurry.

Buster

Buster took a careful peek
over the edge.

"Whoa! That's a big drop! Hey, guys,
I can show you a quicker way up."

"Thanks, Buster," said Isabelle, "but
we're not looking for the quick way."

"That would take all the fun out of it,"
said Wilson.

Buster visited a climbing school
with his new friends.

"This is our teacher, Kate," said Lindsey.

"Are you a climbing expert?"
Buster asked.

"I sure am," said Kate.

Buster smiled.
"So you can teach me, too?"

"Absolutely," said Kate.

Dear Francine,

Do you sometimes feel like climbing the walls?

Well, there's really a lot to learn about doing it right.

Buster

Buster tried bouldering first.

He moved one foot sideways
close to the floor.

"Okay," he said, "I have a foothold.
How am I doing?"

"You're doing great," said Wilson.

"What about climbing higher?"
asked Buster.

"First," said Wilson, "make sure you have
a rope around you to be safe.
The person holding it is called a belayer.
Then slowly start lifting yourself up,
one step at a time."

Dear Mr. Ratburn,

I am using chalk here, but not to write on the blackboard.

It helps keep my hands dry while I'm climbing.

Buster

"We're pretty high up now," said Buster.
He looked down. "Um, Wilson,
do some people get scared up here?"

"When I was really little," said Wilson,
"I was terrified of doing this."

"I think I'm frozen," said Buster.
"What should I do?"

"Just say 'take' to your belayer," said Wilson. "And then 'lower.'"

"TAKE!" said Buster. "LOWER!"

A moment later, Buster felt himself going down.

"Wow," he said. "I feel like an astronaut returning to earth."

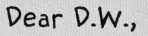

Dear D.W.,

Climbing is safe
if you do it
carefully.

You use ropes
and harnesses
to make sure you
don't fall.

      Buster

Buster still felt nervous at bedtime.

"Even this bed feels a little too high,"
he told his dad. "How can I go to
El Dorado tomorrow?"

"You don't have to go,"
his father reminded him.

"But I want to," said Buster.
"I just don't know what will happen."

That night Buster dreamed
he was climbing El Dorado.

"This is great," he said.
"I'm high up and feel fine."

Suddenly, an eagle swooped down
and carried him off.

"This can't be good," said Buster.

Dear Francine,

Last night I dreamed
I was in a nest with baby eagles.

We all had to eat worms.

In case you were wondering,
worms don't taste good,
even in dreams.

Buster

Francine Frensky
Maple Drive Apt. 5
Elwood City

As Buster approached El Dorado, he tried to prepare himself for the climb.

"I know I'm scared," he thought, "but that's okay."

"I'm sure you can do it," said Kate. "All the kids will help you."

Buster put on his equipment.

"As you climb, put your hands anywhere you can get a good handhold," said Kate.

Dear Binky,

Don't ever try sneaking up
on anyone while you're wearing
rock-climbing equipment.

You'll make way too much noise

Buster

Binky Barnes
10 Pine Tree Road
Elwood City

Buster started to climb.

"Boy, look how high up I am.
Talk about being in a cliff-hanger.
I think I'm at the end of my rope.
Uh-oh, I can't move."

"Take a deep breath and relax,"
said Lindsey.

Dear Muffy,

Did you ever want
a helicopter
to get you out of
a tight spot?

I wish you could
buy me one right
now.

Buster

Dear D.W.,

It is much easier to climb if you keep your eyes open.

But sometimes they seem to shut by themselves.

Buster

D. W. Read
100 Main Street
Elwood City

"Maybe I could move my hand here," Buster began. "And hey. . .this is a good place for my foot."

"You're doing a great job," said Lindsey.

"Keep moving," said Olivia.

Buster could hardly believe it.

"I'm climbing like a spider
straight up the wall.
Hey, guys! I did it!"

Dear Arthur,

I made it to the top of the mountain.

And I even had my eyes open most of the time.

Buster

Buster looked at the mountains
and the climbers around him.

"This is amazing," he said.
"Now I understand why you spend
so much time outside. It feels great
to be out here climbing the rocks
and being part of it all."

Dear Wilson, Lindsey, Olivia, and Isabelle,

The only real climbing I do at home is going up the ladder to Arthur's tree house.

There's a good view from the top.

Buster